CHRISTMAS JOKES FOR KIDS AGE 5-12

Over 200 Fun Jokes About Santa Claus, Reindeer, Elves, Stockings, Snow Days, and Carols

Mahdi Amini

Cover design by: Canvas

Introduction

Welcome, dear readers! If you're seeking a thrilling escape into the world of stories for kids and adults or if you're in the market for beautifully designed notebooks, I invite you to visit my author page. It's your gateway to a realm of chilling narratives and exquisite stationery. Thank you "Mahdi Amini"

Contents

Christmas Characters And Events

1. Santa Claus: Santa Claus, also known as Saint Nicholas, is the jolly man in the red suit who brings gifts to children all around the world on Christmas Eve. Kids eagerly await his arrival, leaving out milk and cookies for him.

2. Reindeer: Santa's sleigh is pulled by a team of magical reindeer, including Rudolph with his shiny red nose. Children love stories about Santa's reindeer and their adventures.

3. Elves: Santa's little helpers, the elves, work diligently at the North Pole to make toys for children. Kids enjoy stories about their mischievous antics and their role in preparing for Christmas.

4. Christmas Tree: Decorating the Christmas tree is a cherished tradition. Kids love hanging ornaments, tinsel, and lights on the tree. They also look forward to the moment when the tree is lit for the first time.

5. Christmas Carols: Singing Christmas carols is a fun activity for kids. They enjoy learning the lyrics to classics like "Jingle Bells" and "Deck the Halls."

6. Gingerbread Houses: Building and decorating gingerbread houses is a creative and tasty Christmas tradition. Kids love making their own gingerbread creations.

7. Advent Calendar: Advent calendars help kids count down the days until Christmas. They open a little door or pocket each day to reveal a surprise or treat.

8. Letters to Santa: Many children write letters to Santa, sharing their Christmas wishes. It's a delightful way to express their hopes for the holiday.

9. Christmas Movies: Watching classic Christmas movies like "A Christmas Carol," "The Polar Express," and "Home Alone" is a favorite holiday pastime for kids.

10. Christmas Stockings: Kids hang stockings by the fireplace, hoping that Santa will fill them with small gifts and goodies.

11. Christmas Cookies: Baking and decorating Christmas cookies is a delightful activity for kids. They get to enjoy the sweet treats they help create.

12. Snow Days: In regions with winter snow, kids eagerly await the possibility of a "white Christmas" and enjoy playing in the snow, building snowmen, and having snowball fights.

13. Holiday Lights: Many families take drives to see beautifully decorated houses and streets with colorful holiday lights.

Santa Claus Jokes

Why did Santa go to music school? Because he wanted to improve his "wrap" skills!

What does Santa use to take attendance at the North Pole? His "naughty or nice"book!

What do you call Santa when he takes a break? Santa Pause!

What did Santa say to the smoker? Please don't smoke, it's bad for my "elf"!

Why did Santa bring a ladder to Christmas? Because he wanted to go "up on the housetop"!

What do you call Santa when he takes a nap? Santa Snooze!

What do you get if you cross Santa with a detective? Santa Clues!

Why did Santa go to the doctor? Because he had Claus-trophobia!

What do you call Santa when he loses his pants? Saint Knickerless!

What do you get if you cross Santa with a detective? Santa Clues!

What kind of music do you listen to at Christmas? "Wrap" music!

Why was Santa's math book so sad? Because it had too many problems!

What do you call Santa when he acts up? Santa Jaws!

What do you get when you cross a snowman and a vampire? Frostbite!

Why was Santa's computer so slow? Because it had too many "chimney" bytes!

What do you get if you cross Santa with a detective? Santa Clues!

What do you get if you cross Santa with a baker? Krisp Kringles!

What does Santa use to stay safe in the sun? "Santa"-screen!

What does Santa use to bake cookies? His "elf"-raising flour!

Why did Santa bring a ladder to the Christmas party? Because he wanted to go "up on the rooftop, click, click, click"!

Reindeer Jokes

What do you call a reindeer with no eyes?

No-eye-deer!

Why did Rudolph get a ticket?

He was parked in a "no sleighing" zone!

What do you get if you cross a snowman and a reindeer?

Frostbite!

What did one reindeer say to the other?

"I don't know, I thought you knew the way!"

What's a reindeer's favorite game?

"Freeze tag"!

Why don't reindeer play cards in the wild?

Because there are too many cheetahs!

What do you get if you cross a reindeer and an elephant?

An eight-foot-tall reindeer with a large trunk!

What's a reindeer's favorite candy?

Jolly "Hoof" Day candies!

What's a reindeer's favorite type of dance?

The "hoof-step"!

What do you get when you cross a reindeer with a detective?

Reindeer sleuth!

Why did the reindeer bring a ladder to Christmas?

Because it wanted to go "up on the housetop"!

What do reindeer use to decorate their Christmas tree?

"Horn"-aments!

What did one reindeer say to the other when they saw the presents?

"Hoof" do you think they got here?"

Why was the reindeer at the beach?

He wanted to play in the "rein"sand!

How does a reindeer keep its fur looking nice?

It uses "antler" spray!

What do you call a reindeer who tells jokes?

A "comedi-deer"!

Why did the reindeer cross the road?

To prove it could be done!

What do you call a reindeer with no manners?

"Rude"-olph!

What do you call a reindeer with a GPS?

"Rudolph the Red-Nosed Navigator"!

What's a reindeer's favorite treat?

Candy "cane"-es!

Elves jokes

Why did the Christmas elf go to school?

To get "elf"-ucated!

What do you call an elf who sings?

An "elf"-abet!

What do you call an elf who tells jokes?

A "punch-line" elf!

What did one elf say to the other?

"I'm a little short!"

Why did the elf put his bed in the fireplace?

He wanted to sleep like a "yule" log!

How do you greet an elf on the shelf?

"Ello there!"

What's an elf's favorite kind of music?

"Wrap" music!

What do you call an elf who loves to take baths?

A "self-cleaning" elf!

How do you make an elf laugh on Christmas?

Tell them your "elf"-standing jokes!

Why was the elf always in trouble at school?

Because he had "elf"-ish behavior!

How do you know if an elf is good at karate?

He has a "black elf" belt!

What do you call an elf who tells secrets?

A "Santa's little whisperer"!

Why did the elf bring a ladder to the North Pole?

He heard the North Pole was a bit "elevated"!

What's an elf's favorite type of math?

"Wrap"-lication!

How does an elf greet you during

the holiday season?

With "elf"-esteem!

Why do elves make terrible spies?

Because they're always short on cover!

What do you get when you cross an elf with a kangaroo?

A "krisp-y kanga-elf"!

Why did the elf take a ladder to the cookie jar?

Because he wanted to try a "high" dive!

How do you get an elf to stop using your computer?

Install "elf-er" protection!

Why did the elf bring a pencil to the toy factory?

He wanted to "elf"-abetize the toy list!

Christmas Tree Jokes

Why was the Christmas tree so bad at sewing?

It couldn't thread the needle!

What do you call a tree that loves to knit?

A "purl" tree!

Why did the Christmas tree go to the barber?

It needed a trim!

What's a Christmas tree's favorite candy?

Orna-"mint"s!

What did the Christmas tree say to the ornament?

"You make me feel so tree-mendous!"

Why was the Christmas tree always in trouble?

Because it couldn't stop branching out!

What's a tree's favorite dance?

The tree-step!

Why did the Christmas tree bring a ladder to the forest?

It wanted to visit its family tree!

What's a tree's least favorite month?

Sep-"timber"!

What do you call a tree that tells jokes?

A "comedy" tree!

Why did the Christmas tree go to the doctor?

It was feeling a bit "sappy"!

How does a tree get on the internet?

It logs in!

What did one Christmas tree say to the other?

"You're pining for attention!"

How do you catch a squirrel from a Christmas tree?

Climb up and act like a nut!

Why did the Christmas tree want to be a musician?

It wanted to be "evergreen" in the charts!

What did the decorator say to the Christmas tree?

"You look tree-mendous in those ornaments!"

Why was the Christmas tree a great listener?

It had good "tree"-spection!

What's a tree's favorite board game?

"Tree-go"!

Why don't Christmas trees knit scarves?

They're afraid of the "yarn" ball!

What do you call a tree that's always cold?

A "brrr"-ch!

Christmas Caroles jokes

Why did the carolers go to school?

To "sleigh" their singing lessons!

What's a caroler's favorite kind of pizza?

"Wrap"-peroni!

How do you make a carol stop singing?

Take away its "tinsel"!

What do you call a snowman who loves to sing carols?

"Frosty the Singer"!

Why did the carolers bring a ladder to the concert?

They wanted to reach the high notes!

What do you call a carol that tells jokes?

A "comedy" carol!

Why did the carolers bring a vacuum to the holiday party?

They wanted to clean up the "snow-tations"!

What's a caroler's favorite type of music?

"Wrap" music!

How does a snowman sing carols?

With "ice" pitch!

Why was the Christmas carol feeling chilly?

It had too many "brrr"-est notes!

What do you get if you cross a snowman and a caroler?

Frosty the "Melody"!

Why did the caroler bring a ladder to the Christmas tree?

To reach the "high" notes!

What do you call a carol that loves to eat?

A "jelly-roll" carol!

What's a caroler's favorite place in the house?

The "wreath"-room!

Why did the carolers use a calendar when singing?

They wanted to be "date"-perfect!

What did the caroler say to the snowman?

"You're the coolest audience ever!"

How do you make a tissue dance to a Christmas carol?

You put a little "boogie" in it!

Why was the Christmas carol feeling so festive?

It was in the "holly"-day spirit!

What's a caroler's favorite type of math?

"Wrap"-geometry!

What do you call a carol that goes to the beach?

A "seashell"-er!

Gingerbread Houses jokes

What do you get when you cross a gingerbread house with a snowman? Frostbite!

How do you fix a broken gingerbread house? With icing and gumdrops, of course!

What's a gingerbread house's favorite music? "Icing, Icing Baby!"

Why was the gingerbread house always calm and collected? Because it had great frosting!

What do gingerbread houses use to repair their roofs? Icing shingles!

How do gingerbread houses stay warm in the winter? They use gingerbread heaters!

What do you call a gingerbread house on a diet? A ginger "bread" house!

What did the gingerbread house say to the gingerbread man? "You're icing-tastic!"

Why did the gingerbread house go to the doctor? It was feeling crumby!

What do you call a gingerbread house that tells jokes? A pun-derful home!

How does a gingerbread house stay in shape? It uses ginger-aerobics!

What do gingerbread houses hang on their walls? Cookie frames!

Why do gingerbread houses make great detectives? They always have their cookie eyes on the suspects!

What's a gingerbread house's favorite TV show? "The Great British Bake Off"!

Why don't gingerbread houses ever win at hide-and-seek? They always crumble under pressure!

How do gingerbread houses send mail? With chocolate-chip stamps, of course!

What's a gingerbread house's favorite game? Candy Land!

What's a gingerbread house's favorite song during the holidays? "I'm Dreaming of a White (Icing) Christmas"!

What do you call a gingerbread house that's full of holiday spirit? "Ginger-jolly"!

Why did the gingerbread house invite the gingerbread man for tea? Because it wanted to have a sweet conversation!

Advent Calendar jokes

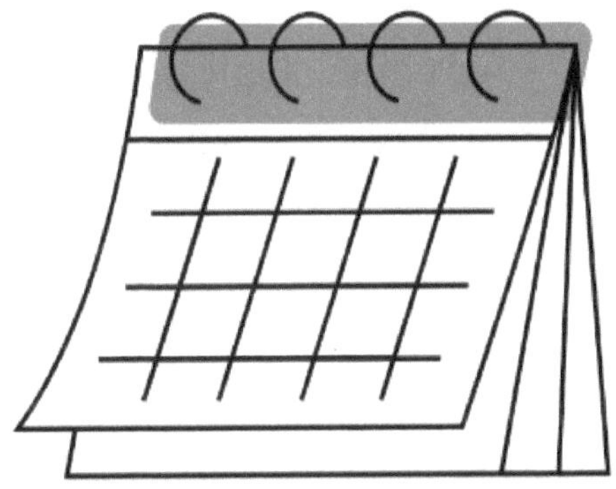

What do you call an Advent Calendar that tells jokes? A "laughs-of-the-day" calendar!

Why did the snowman open his Advent Calendar early? He just couldn't "frost" resist!

How do you know when it's time to open the Advent Calendar? When it's "dates" to start!

What did the reindeer find in their Advent Calendar? Santa "clues"!

Why did the gingerbread cookie refuse to open the Advent Calendar? It was afraid of "crumby" jokes!

What's the Advent Calendar's favorite holiday season? "Counting"-mas!

Why did the elf bring a ladder to the Advent Calendar? Because he wanted to "climb-bell" to the best treats!

What do you call an Advent Calendar that plays music? A "tune"-box calendar!

Why was the Christmas tree so good at opening the Advent Calendar? Because it had "branch" power!

How does the snowman know which day of the Advent Calendar

it is? He checks the "snow-date"!

What's the best way to eat chocolate from the Advent Calendar? In a "yule-log" manner!

Why did the gingerbread person start a band with their Advent Calendar chocolates? Because they wanted to make "sweet" music!

How did the Advent Calendar prepare for its grand opening? It had a "count"-down party!

What's a snowman's favorite treat from the Advent Calendar? "Melt"-ed chocolate!

Why did the Christmas lights decorate the Advent Calendar? Because they wanted to add some "sparkle" to the countdown!

What do you call a holiday surprise hidden in the Advent Calendar? A "calendar-copter"!

What did the ornament say when it got stuck in the Advent Calendar door? "I'm bauble to get out!"

Why did the reindeer bring a calendar to the North Pole? Because Santa needed a "sleigh" schedule!

How does the Advent Calendar send holiday greetings? It "opens" up to new possibilities!

What's the best Advent Calendar joke for Christmas Eve? A "punchline" that's right on schedule!

Letters To Santa Jokes

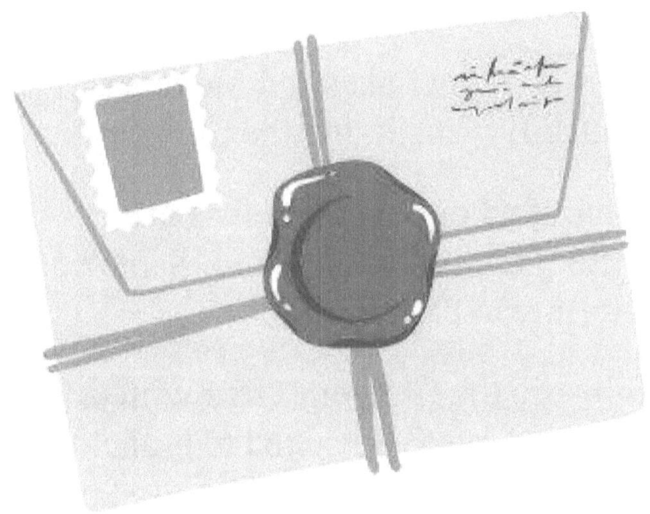

Why did the computer send a letter to Santa? Because it wanted a new "mouse"!

What did the pencil say to the paper when writing its letter to Santa? "You're stationery!"

What do you get if you cross a snowman with a vampire while writing a letter to Santa? Frostbite!

How do snowflakes send letters to Santa? By "mail"-ing them!

What kind of paper do elves use to write their letters to Santa? Shortbread paper!

Why did the Christmas tree write a letter to Santa? It wanted to branch out its wishes!

How do reindeer sign their letters to Santa? With hoofprints!

What's Santa's favorite part of receiving letters from kids? "Reindeer" messages!

What's the secret ingredient in Santa's favorite cookies? North "pole"-enta!

Why did the gingerbread person send Santa a letter? To "sweeten" the holiday deal!

What do you get when you cross a snowman and a dog writing a letter to Santa? Frostbite with a "bite"!

How do Santa's elves address their letters to the North Pole? With an "ice" stamp!

Why did the candy cane write a letter to Santa? To share its "stri-peas"!

How do you send a letter to Santa via email? You "wrap" it in an attachment!

What's the best way to make sure Santa reads your letter? Seal it with a "snow-kiss"!

What's the fastest way to deliver a letter to Santa? Use a "sleigh"mail service!

What's Santa's favorite letter-opening tool? His "claws" on Christmas Eve!

What kind of stamp does a snowman use on its letter to Santa? A "frost-class" stamp!

Why did the snow globe write a letter to Santa? It wanted to "shake up" the holiday season!

What did the stocking say to Santa in its letter? "I'm "hanging" around for your gifts!"

Christmas Movies Jokes

Why did the Christmas tree go to the movies? It wanted to be a "tree star" on the big screen!

What's a snowman's favorite Christmas movie? "Frosted" the Snowman!

What did one ornament say to the

other while watching a Christmas movie? "You're such a ball!"

Why did the gingerbread cookie refuse to watch holiday films? It was afraid of getting "crumby" ideas!

What do you call a snowman who loves action-packed Christmas movies? Frosty "the Explosive" Snowman!

Why do elves love watching Christmas movies on DVD? Because they can "unwrap" the fun again and again!

How do you catch a squirrel that's interrupting your Christmas movie marathon? Climb a tree and "nut"-work the problem!

What do you get if you cross a reindeer with a movie director during the holidays? A "cinema-deer"!

What's a Christmas elf's favorite movie snack? "Elfish" pretzels!

How do you make an impression at a Christmas movie party? Bring a "snow-stopping" appetizer!

Why was the scarecrow watching Christmas movies in the field? It wanted to learn the "ropes"!

What kind of music do Santa's reindeer like to dance to after a movie night? "Sleigh-hop"!

What's a snowman's favorite actor in Christmas movies? Frost "Globeson"!

What did one snowflake say to the other while watching a holiday film? "Isn't this flake-tastic?"

What's the best way to enjoy a Christmas movie marathon? With a "blizzard" of blankets and hot cocoa!

Why do Christmas lights love watching movies? They're always "lit" for the show!

How do you make sure your favorite Christmas movie doesn't disappear? You "freeze" the frame!

What's a penguin's favorite Christmas movie? "Chill" Bill!

Why did the Christmas tree attend a movie casting call? It wanted to be the star of the show!

What do you get if you cross a snowball with a film projector? A "snow-show" of a movie night!

Christmas Stockings Jokes

Why did the Christmas stocking go to the North Pole? To visit its "stock-ing" stuffer friends!

What did one Christmas stocking say to the other? "We make quite the 'pair'!"

Why did the elf bring a ladder to the Christmas stocking factory? He wanted to "climb" the corporate "stuffer"!

How does a Christmas stocking keep its feet warm in the winter? It wears "stocking" caps!

What's a snowman's favorite stocking stuffer? An "ice-sicle"!

Why did the Christmas stocking visit the cookie factory? It wanted to find some "sweet" treats!

What do you call a Christmas stocking that's also a musician? A "stocking" note!

How do you know when a Christmas stocking is telling you a joke? It's "seam"-ple, it'll have you in stitches!

What do you get if you cross a Christmas stocking with a rocket? A "stuffer" that's out of this world!

Why did the Christmas stocking go to the doctor? It had a bad case of "stocking-itis"!

What's a Christmas stocking's favorite dance? The "stocking" stomp!

How do you catch a mischievous Christmas stocking? Use a "stocking" net!

Why did the Christmas stocking

invite all the other stockings to a party? It wanted to have a "knit"-together!

What did one Christmas stocking say to the other in the morning? "I'm feeling 'seam-tastic' today!"

Why did the Christmas stocking apply for a job as Santa's helper? It wanted to be a "stuffer" of dreams!

What's a Christmas stocking's favorite kind of ice cream? "Rocky Road"!

What's a snowman's favorite game to play with stockings? "Freeze" tag!

Why did the Christmas stocking always ace its tests at school? It had a "sock-cessful" study strategy!

How do Christmas stockings stay organized during the holiday season? They use "stock-tickers"!

What did the Christmas stocking say when it got stuck in the chimney? "Oh, 'seam' to be in a tight spot!"

Christmas Cookies Jokes

Why did the gingerbread cookie go to the doctor? It was feeling crumby!

What do you get if you cross a snowman and a vampire cookie? Frostbite!

Why did the chocolate chip cookie go to school? It wanted to be a smart cookie!

What did one cookie say to the other cookie at the Christmas party? "You're so sweet!"

How do you make a gingerbread cookie laugh? Tell it a funny frosting joke!

What do you call a cookie that's on the computer? A "website" cookie!

Why did the cookie go to therapy? It had too many chips on its shoulders!

What kind of cookies do snowmen eat on a hot day? Melted chocolate chip cookies!

What's a Christmas tree's favorite type of cookie? Pine-nut!

Why was the sugar cookie feeling grumpy? It needed a little sugar rush!

How do you make a gingerbread cookie house? With lots of elbow grease!

What's a vampire's favorite Christmas cookie? I-scream cookies!

What did the gingerbread man use

to fix his house? Icing and gumdrops!

Why did the cookie cry? Because its mother was a wafer too long!

How do you make a gingerbread cookie giggle? Tickle its raisin buttons!

What do you call a snowman's favorite cookie? Frosted flakes!

Why did the cookie apply for a job? It wanted to make lots of dough!

What did the cookie say to the butter? "You make me melt!"

How do you know a cookie is a math expert? It can count its chocolate chips!

What's a reindeer's favorite type of cookie? One with deer frosting!

Snow Days Jokes

Why did the snowman bring a broom to the snow day? Because he wanted to clean up his act!

What do you call a snowman in the summer? A puddle!

Why did the snowflake bring a notebook to school? To take notes in ice-ology class!

What did one snowflake say to the other? "You're one in a million!"

How do you catch a snowflake? With a butterfly net!

Why did the snowman call his friend an "ice" guy? Because he was so cool!

What do you get if you cross a snowman and a vampire? Frostbite!

What do you call a snowman party? A "snowball!"

What do you call a snowman with

a six-pack? An "ab"-ominable snowman!

What did the snowman say to the aggressive carrot? "Get out of my face!"

What do snowmen use to keep their pants up? An "ice" belt!

Why did the snowman wear a hat? Because it was "cool" fashion!

How do you send a letter to a snowman? Drop it in the mailbox when it's snowing!

What do you call a snowman who tells jokes? A "snow"-comedian!

How do you organize a fantastic snowball fight? Roll with it!

What's a snowman's favorite movie? "Freeze Willy"!

What's a snowflake's favorite hobby? I-skiing!

What do snowmen do on Christmas? Chill out!

How does a snowman get around? By riding an "ice"-cycle!

Why was the snowman looking through the carrots? He was picking his nose!

Holiday Lights Jokes

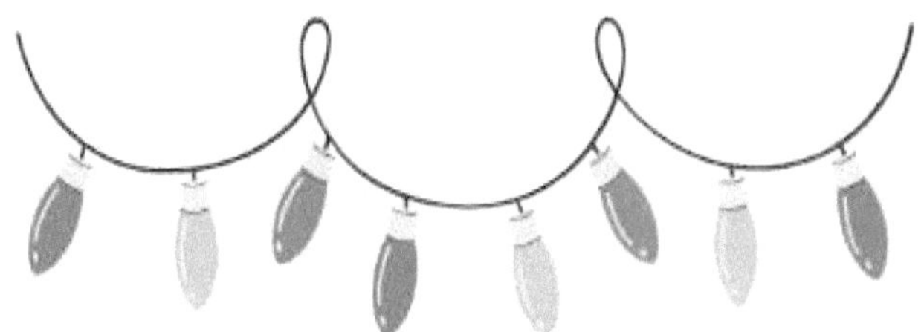

Why did the Christmas lights go to school? Because they wanted to get a little brighter!

How do Christmas lights stay cool? They have "watt"-er cooling!

What did one Christmas light say to the other? "You light up my life!"

What do you call a bulb that doesn't

work? A "dim"-wit!

How do Christmas lights flirt? They make each other "sparkle" with compliments!

What do you get if you cross a snowman and a string of lights? Frostbite!

Why did the Christmas lights keep flickering? They were trying to have a "light"-hearted conversation!

What's a light's favorite holiday song? "Watt Child Is This?"

How do you make a string of Christmas lights happy? Give it a "twinkle" of affection!

What do you call Santa when he takes a break from delivering gifts to admire the lights? Santa Paws!

Why did the Christmas lights get an award? Because they had great "spark-ticipation"!

What's a light's favorite subject in school? "Illumi-nation"!

How do Christmas lights stay in shape? They do "light" aerobics!

What's a light's favorite type of dance? The "wattz"!

What did one Christmas light say to the

other when they finished decorating the tree? "We make a 'brilliant' team!"

How do Christmas lights send messages? Through their "watt"-sapp group!

Why did the Christmas light go to the doctor? It had a "socket" problem!

What do you call a light that tells jokes? A "light"-hearted comedian!

What did the Christmas light say to the ornament? "You're so shiny, I'm 'glow'-rious!"

Why was the Christmas light afraid of the dark? It was a "bulb-phobe"!